MOON GIRL AND DEVIL DINOSAUR

LUNELLA LAFAYETTE doesn't really get other kids her age. And they don't get her either. They call her **MOON GIRL** and laugh at her inventions. It doesn't matter anyway – Lunella's just biding her time until she can get into a **REAL** school for genius kids like her. Who needs friends when you have gizmos to build and books to read?

One night, Lunella found a device called the **OMNI-WAVE PROJECTOR.** So cool! She's been looking for something like this for a long time. If only she could just take it back to her lab and study it...

But during gym class, the projector was activated! It created a **TIME PORTAL**. And through the portal came a bunch of cavemen called the **KILLER FOLK!** They want Lunella's projector. Even **WORSE:** chasing after the KILLER FOLK was a **BIG, RED DINOSAUR!**

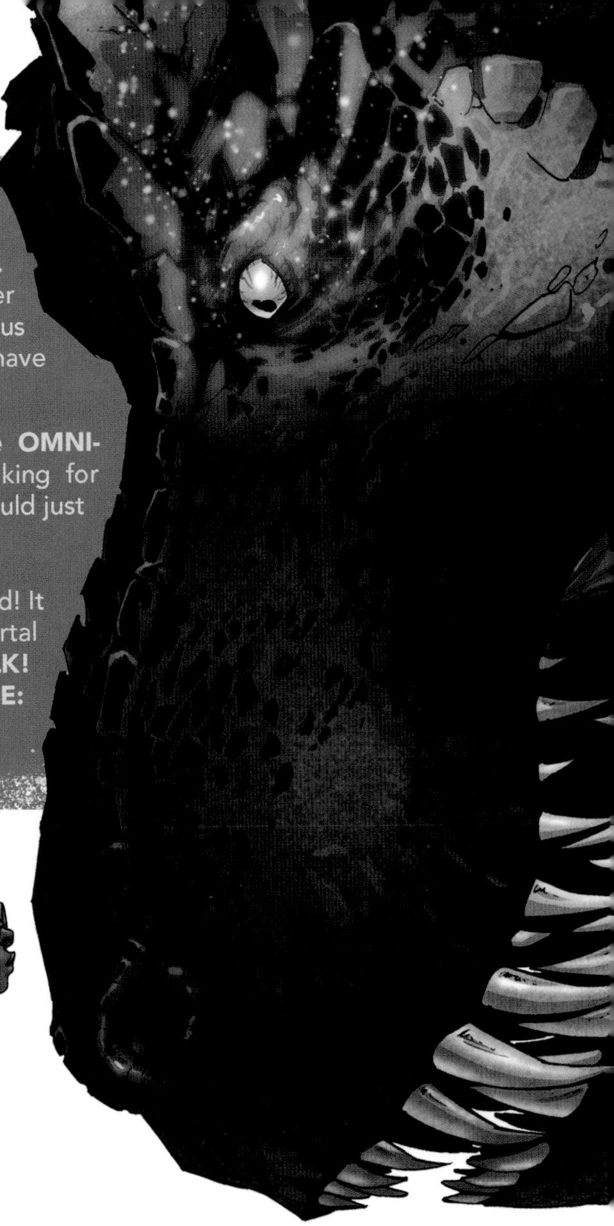

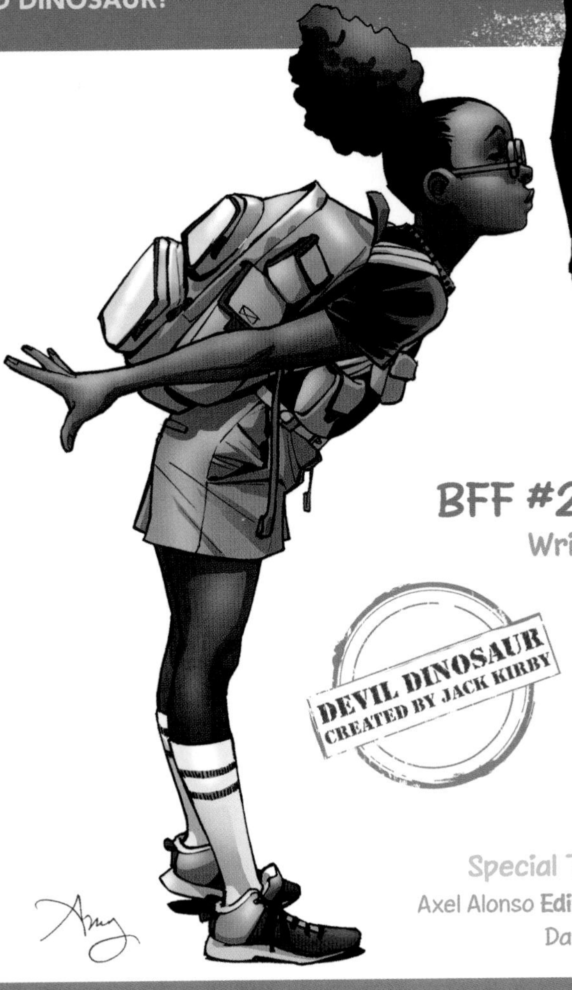
DEVIL DINOSAUR
CREATED BY JACK KIRBY
Amy

BFF #2: Old Dogs and New Tricks

Writers: Brandon Montclare & Amy Reeder
Artist: Natacha Bustos
Colorist: Tamra Bonvillain
Letterer: VC's Travis Lanham
Production Design: Manny Mederos
Editors: Mark Paniccia & Emily Shaw
Cover: Amy Reeder
Variant Cover: Pascal Campion
Special Thanks to Sana Amanat and David Gabriel
Axel Alonso **Editor in Chief** Joe Quesada **Chief Creative Officer**
Dan Buckley **Publisher** Alan Fine **Executive Producer**

ABDOPUBLISHING.COM

Reinforced library bound edition published in 2018 by Spotlight,
a division of ABDO, PO Box 398166, Minneapolis, Minnesota 55439.
Spotlight produces high-quality reinforced library bound editions for
schools and libraries. Published by agreement with Marvel Characters, Inc.

Printed in the United States of America, North Mankato, Minnesota.
042017
092017

THIS BOOK CONTAINS
RECYCLED MATERIALS

MARVEL
marvelkids.com
© 2017 MARVEL

PUBLISHER'S CATALOGING IN PUBLICATION DATA

Names: Reeder, Amy ; Montclare, Brandon, authors. | Bustos, Natacha ; Bonvillain,
    Tamra, illustrators.
Title: Old dogs and new tricks / writers: Amy Reeder ; Brandon Montclare ; art:
    Natacha Bustos ; Tamra Bonvillain.
Description: Reinforced library bound edition. | Minneapolis, Minnesota : Spotlight,
    2018. | Series: Moon Girl and Devil Dinosaur ; BFF #2
Summary: After Lunella teleports a dinosaur and evil humanoids to the middle of
    her gym class, the big dino whisks her off to the city, but when she thinks she's
    safe, the Killer Folk kidnap the super genius.
Identifiers: LCCN 2016961925 | ISBN 9781532140099 (lib. bdg.)
Subjects: LCSH: Schools--Juvenile fiction. | Adventure and adventurers--Juvenile
    fiction. | Comic Books, strips, etc.--Juvenile fiction. | Graphic novels--Juvenile
    fiction.
Classification: DDC 741.5--dc23
LC record available at https://lccn.loc.gov/2016961925

Spotlight

A Division of ABDO
abdopublishing.com

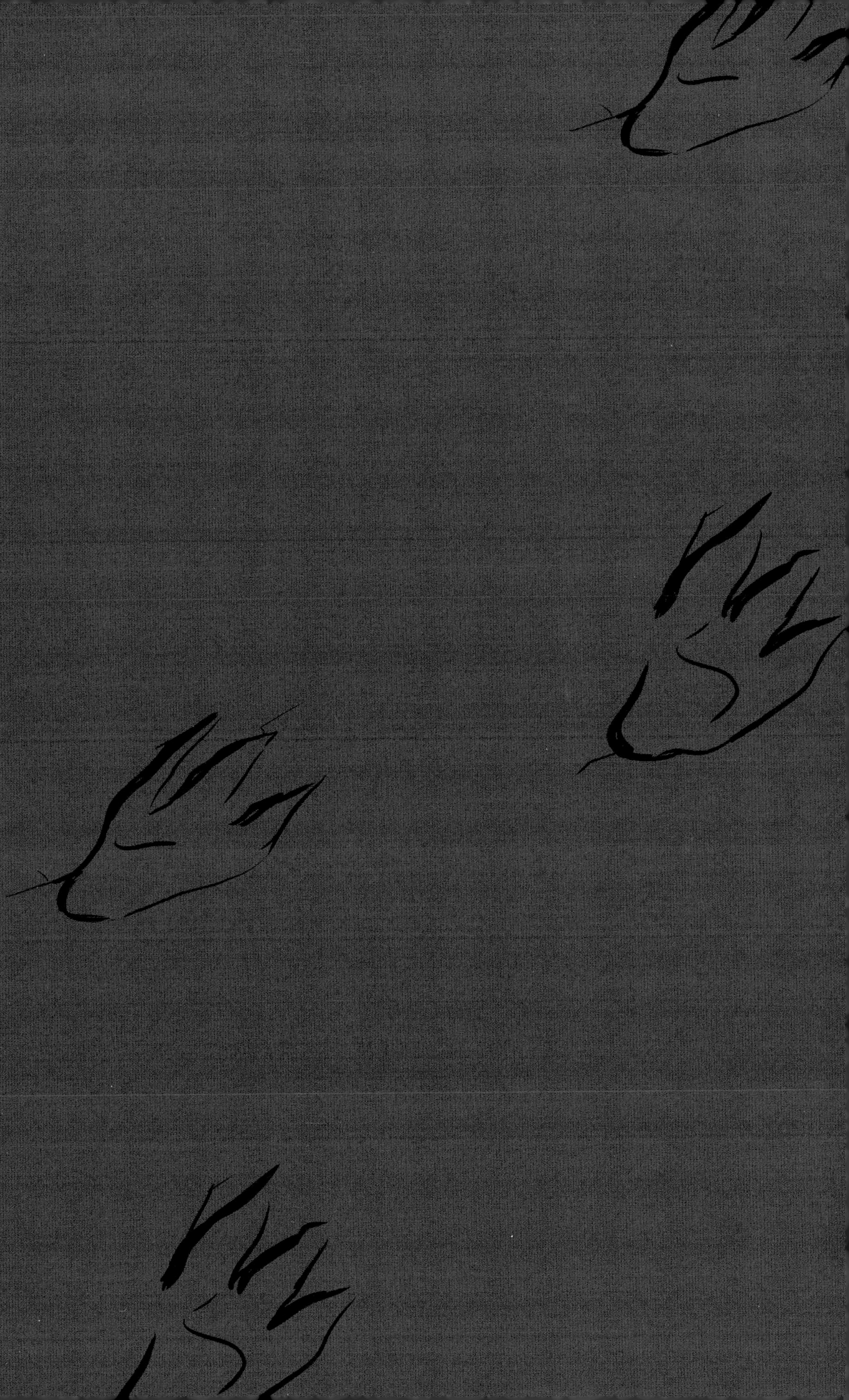

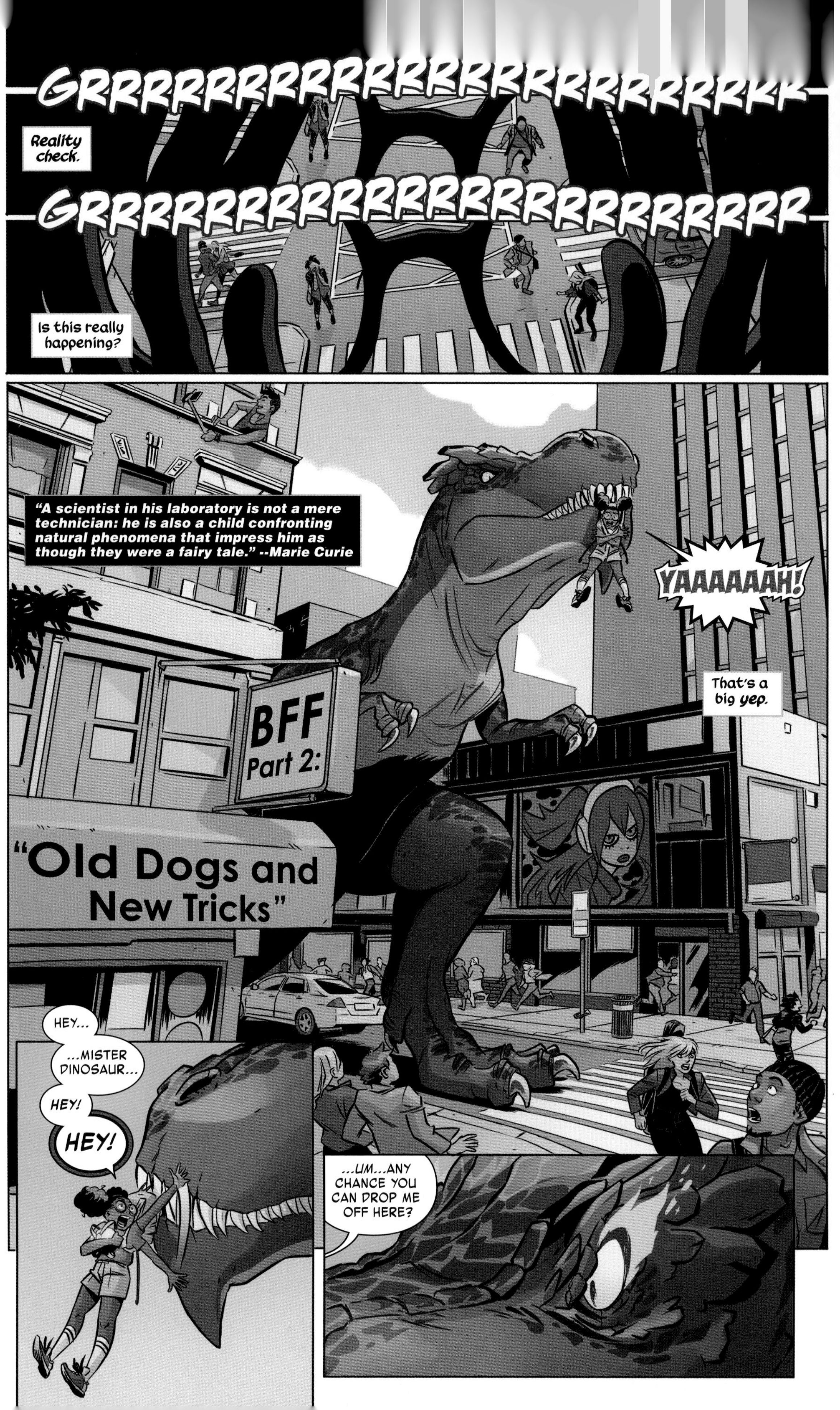
GRRRRRRRRRRRRRRRRRRRRRRR
Reality check.
GRRRRRRRRRRRRRRRRRRRRRRR
Is this really happening?
"A scientist in his laboratory is not a mere technician: he is also a child confronting natural phenomena that impress him as though they were a fairy tale." --Marie Curie
YAAAAAAH!
That's a big yep.
BFF Part 2:
"Old Dogs and New Tricks"
HEY...
...MISTER DINOSAUR...
HEY!
HEY!
...UM...ANY CHANCE YOU CAN DROP ME OFF HERE?

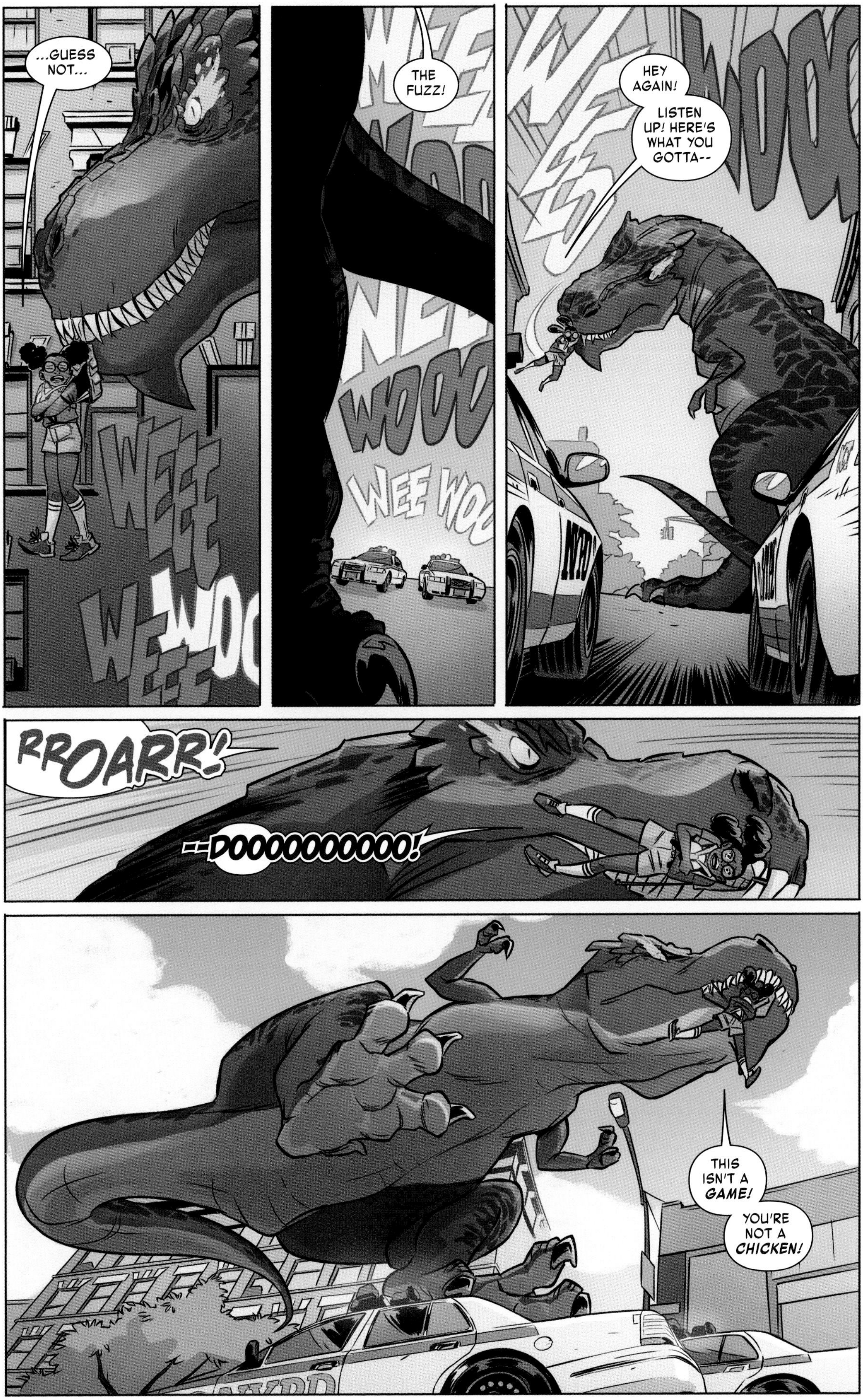

...GUESS NOT...
WEEE
THE FUZZ!
WOOO
WEE WOO
HEY AGAIN!
LISTEN UP! HERE'S WHAT YOU GOTTA--
RROARR!
--DOOOOOOOOOO!
THIS ISN'T A GAME!
YOU'RE NOT A CHICKEN!

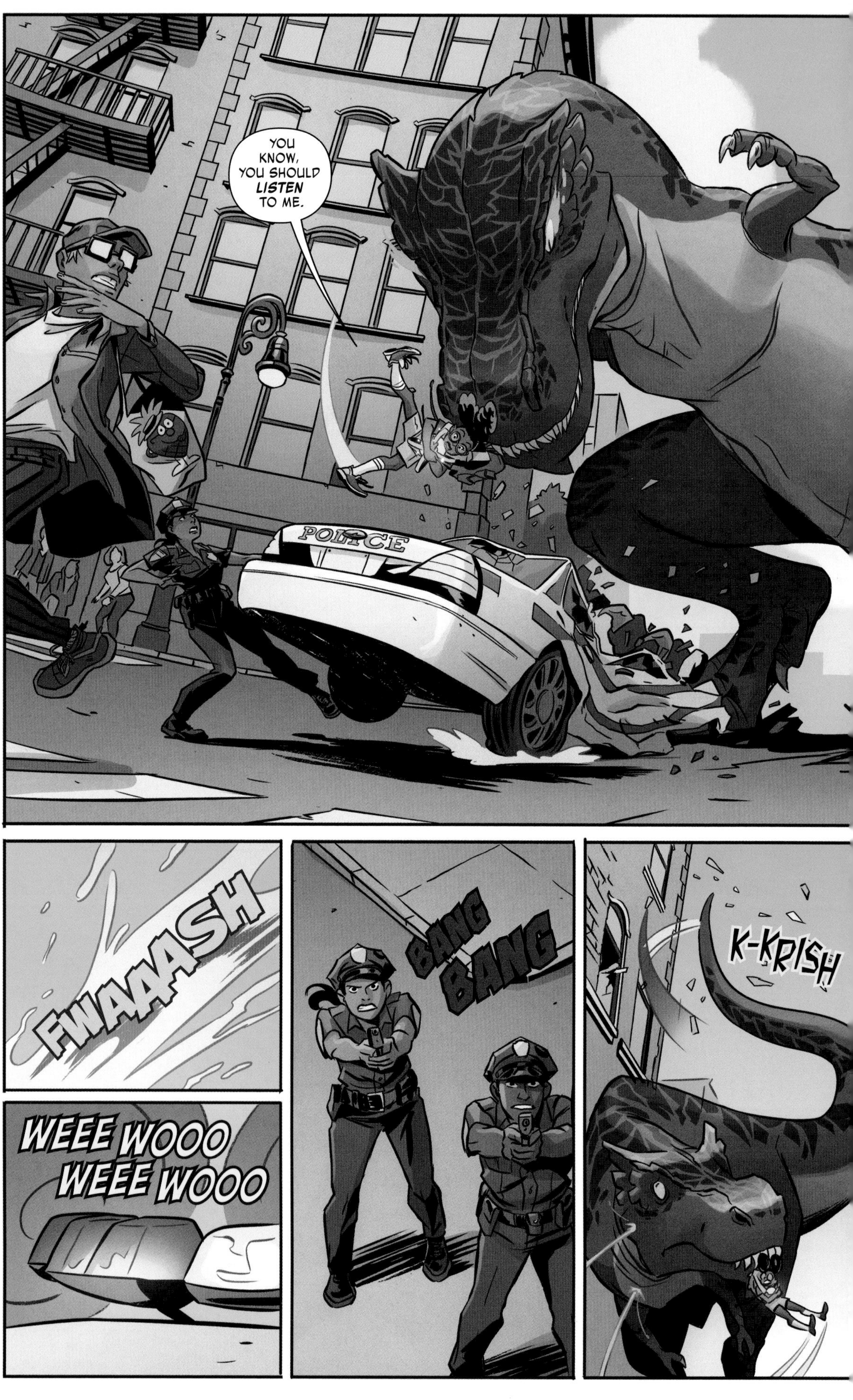
YOU KNOW, YOU SHOULD LISTEN TO ME.
POLICE
FWAAASH
WEEE WOOO
WEEE WOOO
BANG
BANG
K-KRISH

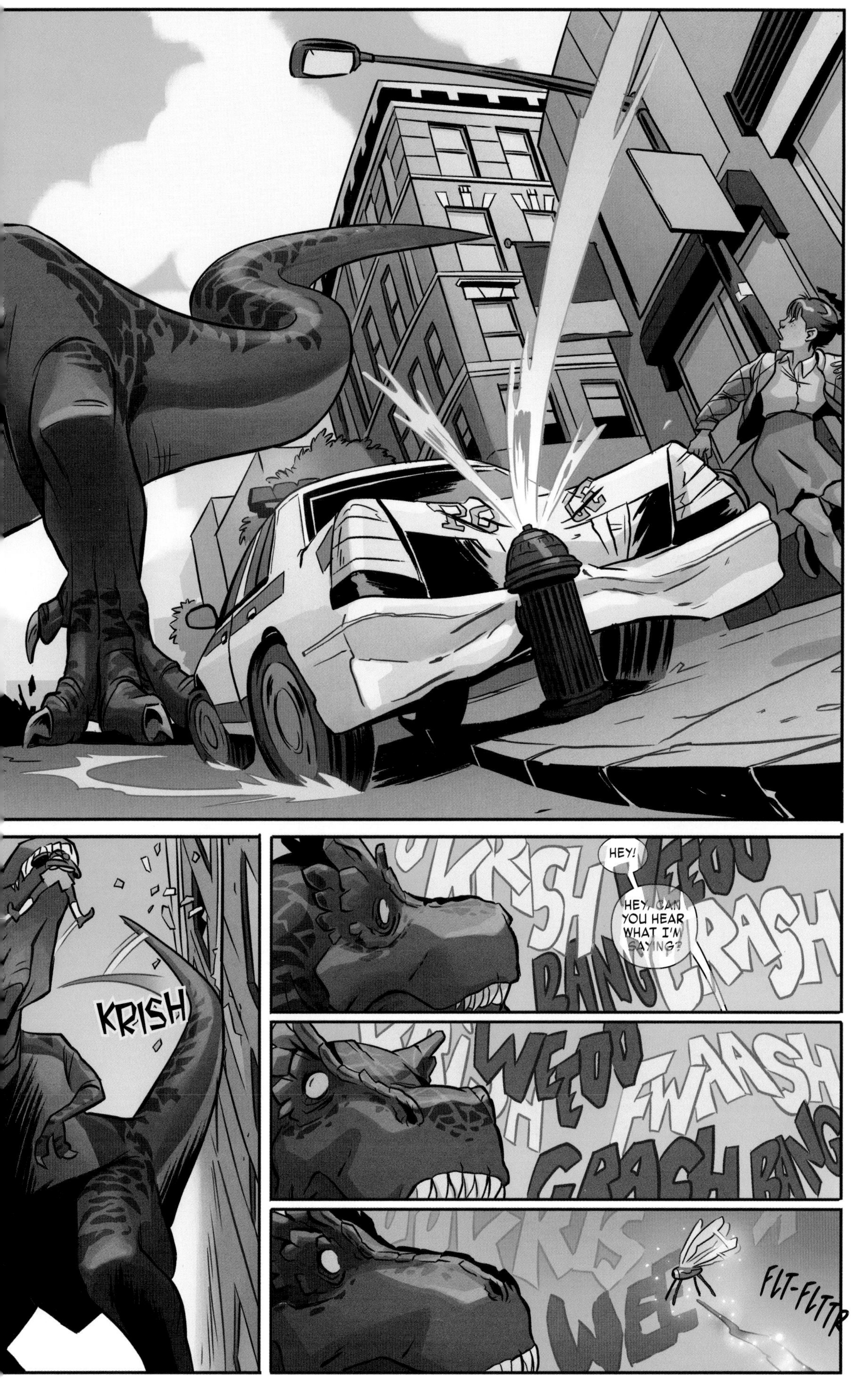
KRISH
HEY!
HEY, CAN YOU HEAR WHAT I'M SAYING?
BANG
CRASH
WEEOO
FWAASH
CRASH
BANG
FLT-FLTTR

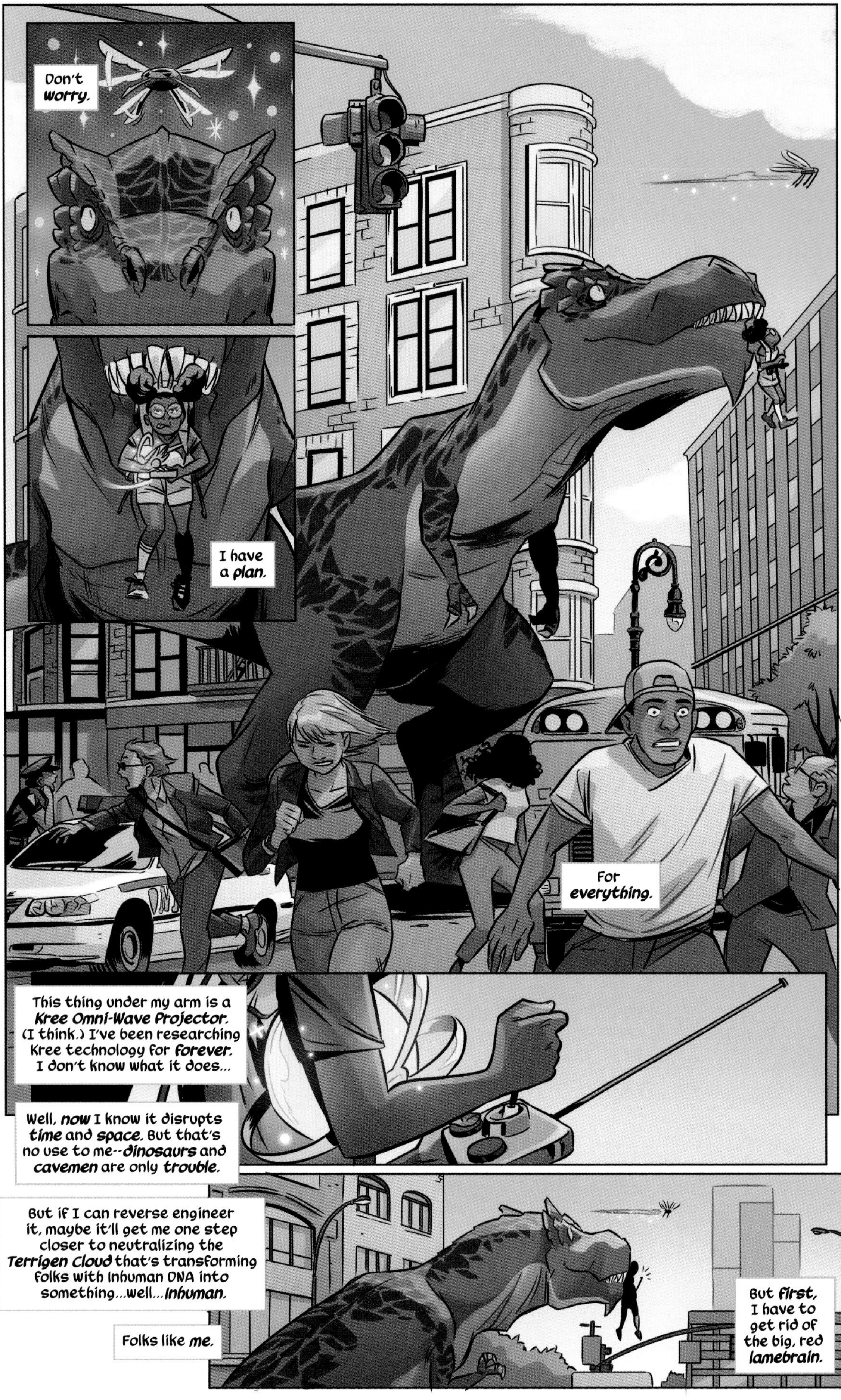
Don't worry.
I have a plan.
For everything.
This thing under my arm is a Kree Omni-Wave Projector. (I think.) I've been researching Kree technology for forever. I don't know what it does...
Well, now I know it disrupts time and space. But that's no use to me--dinosaurs and cavemen are only trouble.
But if I can reverse engineer it, maybe it'll get me one step closer to neutralizing the Terrigen Cloud that's transforming folks with Inhuman DNA into something...well...Inhuman.
Folks like me.
But first, I have to get rid of the big, red lamebrain.

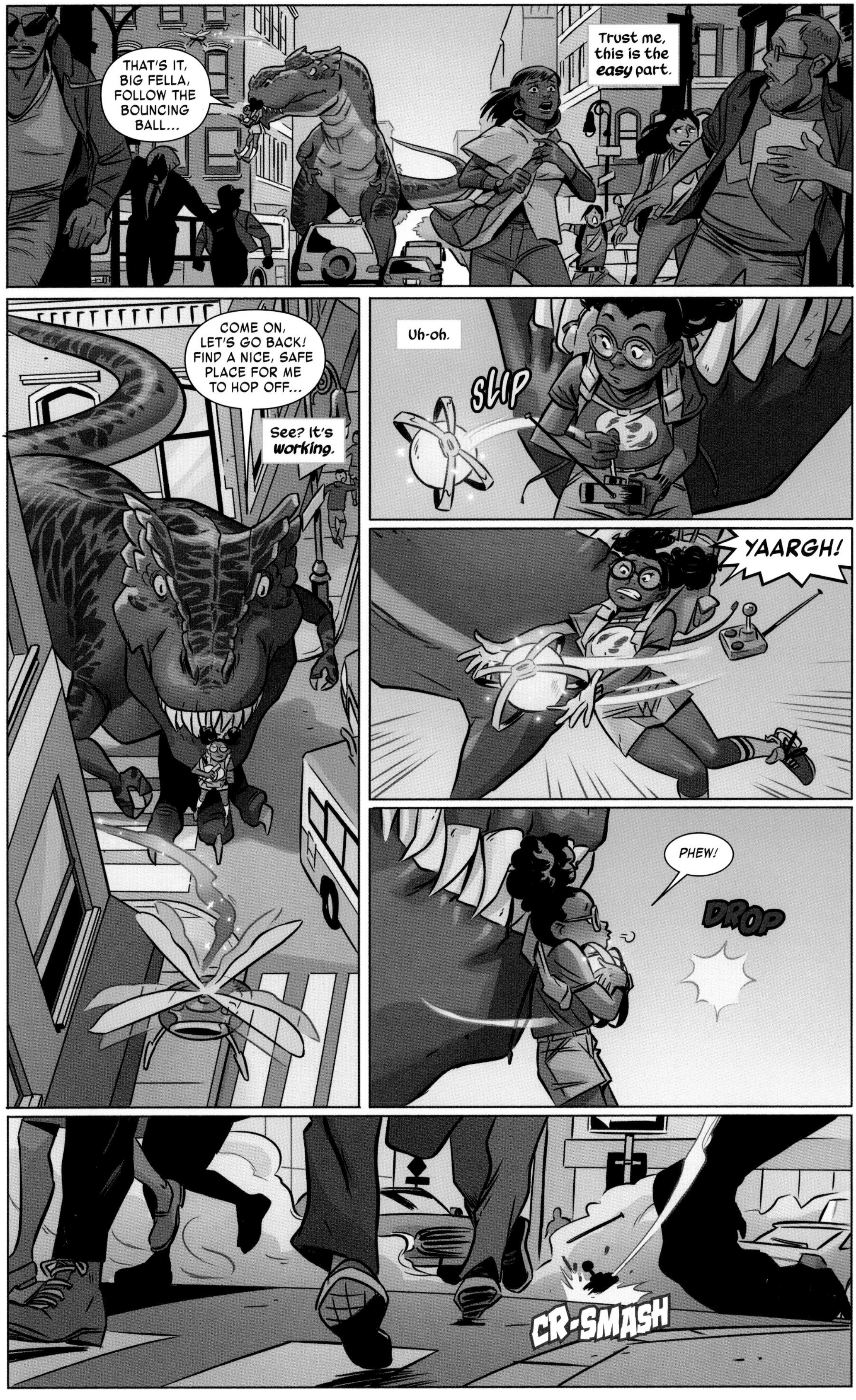
THAT'S IT, BIG FELLA, FOLLOW THE BOUNCING BALL...
Trust me, this is the easy part.
COME ON, LET'S GO BACK! FIND A NICE, SAFE PLACE FOR ME TO HOP OFF...
See? It's working.
Uh-oh.
SLIP
YAARGH!
PHEW!
DROP
CR-SMASH

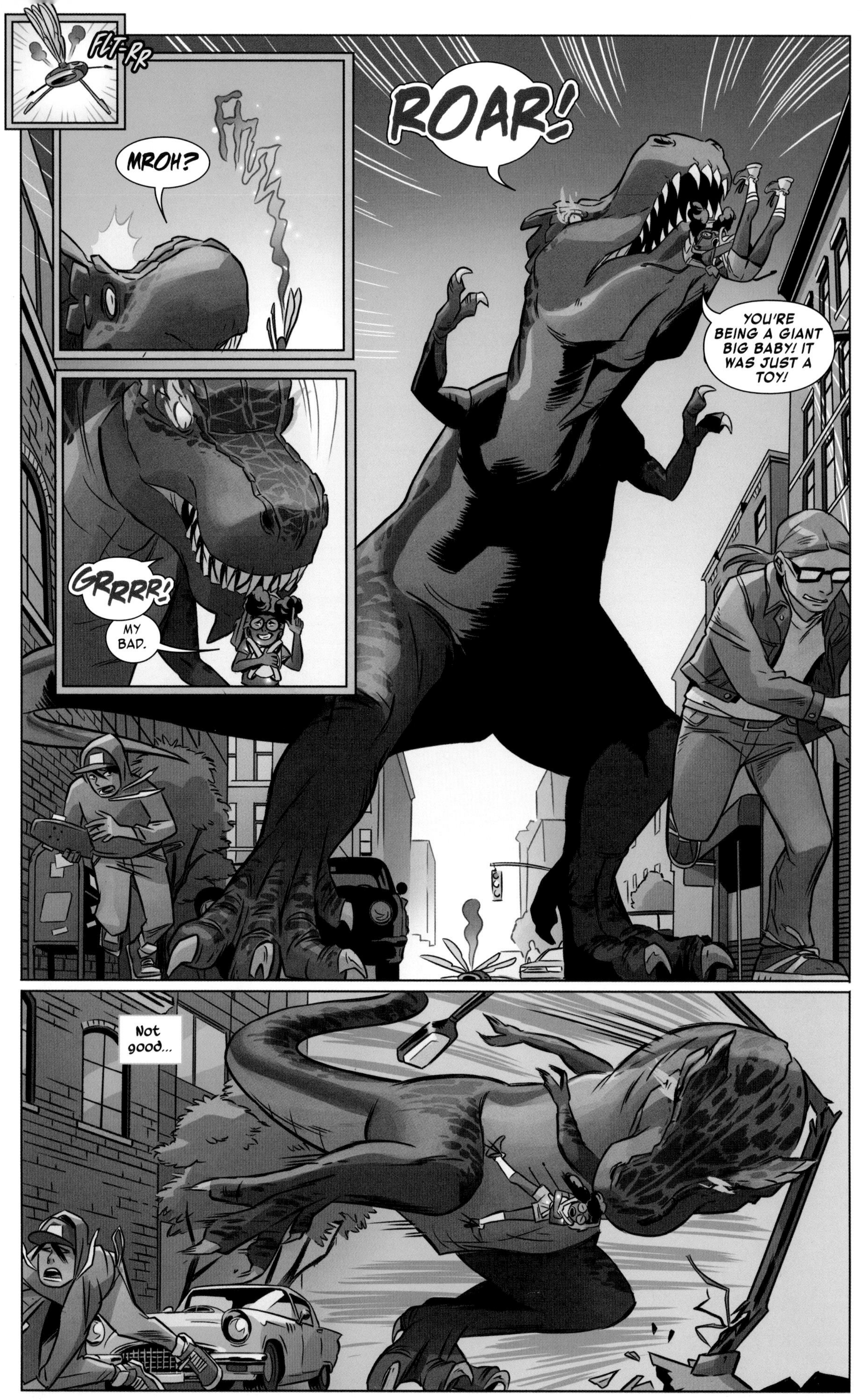
FLT-RR
MROH?
FIZZ
ROAR!
YOU'RE BEING A GIANT BIG BABY! IT WAS JUST A TOY!
GRRRR!
MY BAD.
Not good...

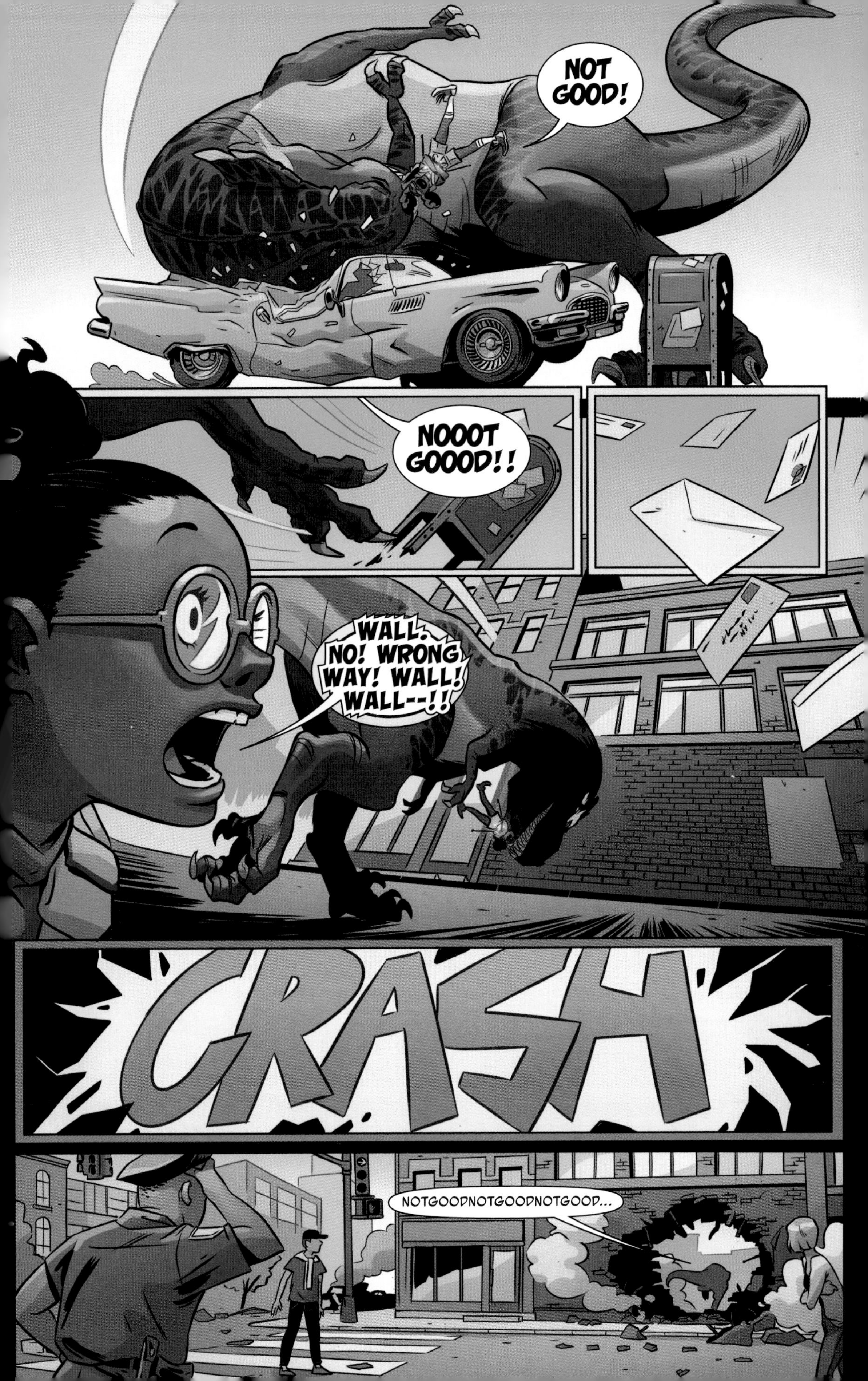
NOT GOOD!
NOOOT GOOOD!!
WALL. NO! WRONG WAY! WALL! WALL--!!
CRASH
NOTGOODNOTGOODNOTGOOD...

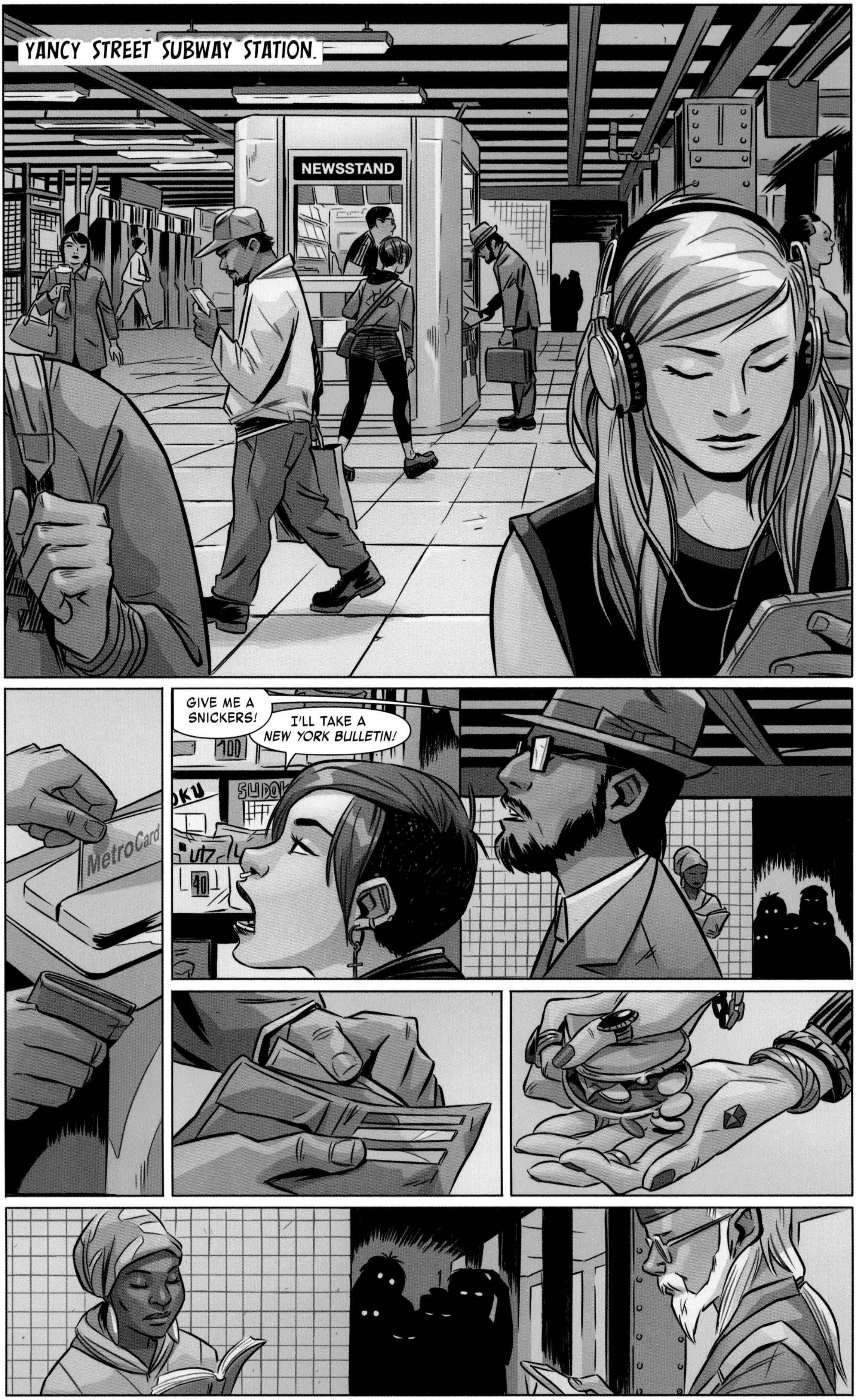
YANCY STREET SUBWAY STATION.
NEWSSTAND
MetroCard
GIVE ME A SNICKERS!
I'LL TAKE A NEW YORK BULLETIN!
SUDOKU

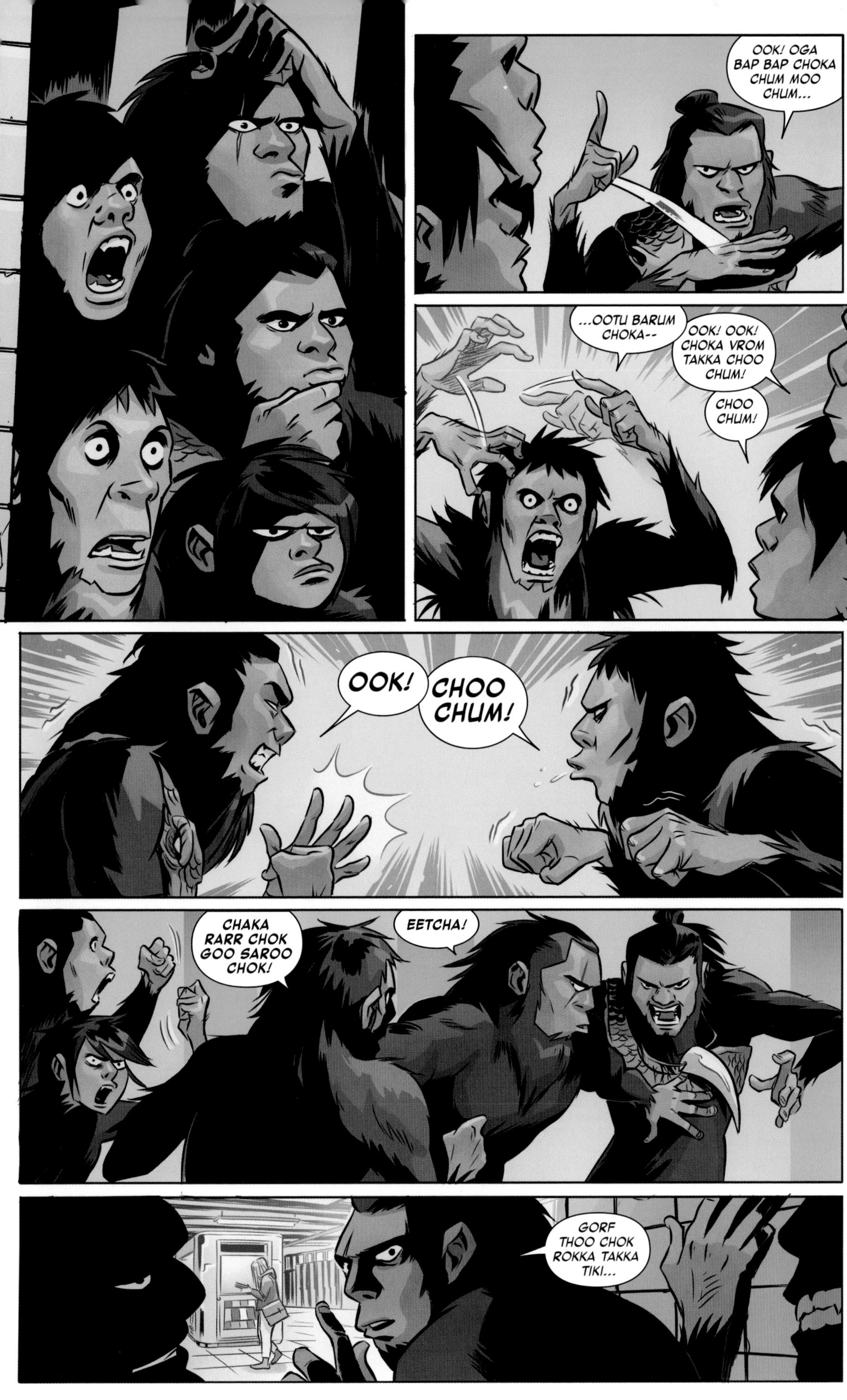
OOK! OGA BAP BAP CHOKA CHUM MOO CHUM...
...OOTU BARUM CHOKA--
OOK! OOK! CHOKA VROM TAKKA CHOO CHUM!
CHOO CHUM!
OOK!
CHOO CHUM!
CHAKA RARR CHOK GOO SAROO CHOK!
EETCHA!
GORF THOO CHOK ROKKA TAKKA TIKI...

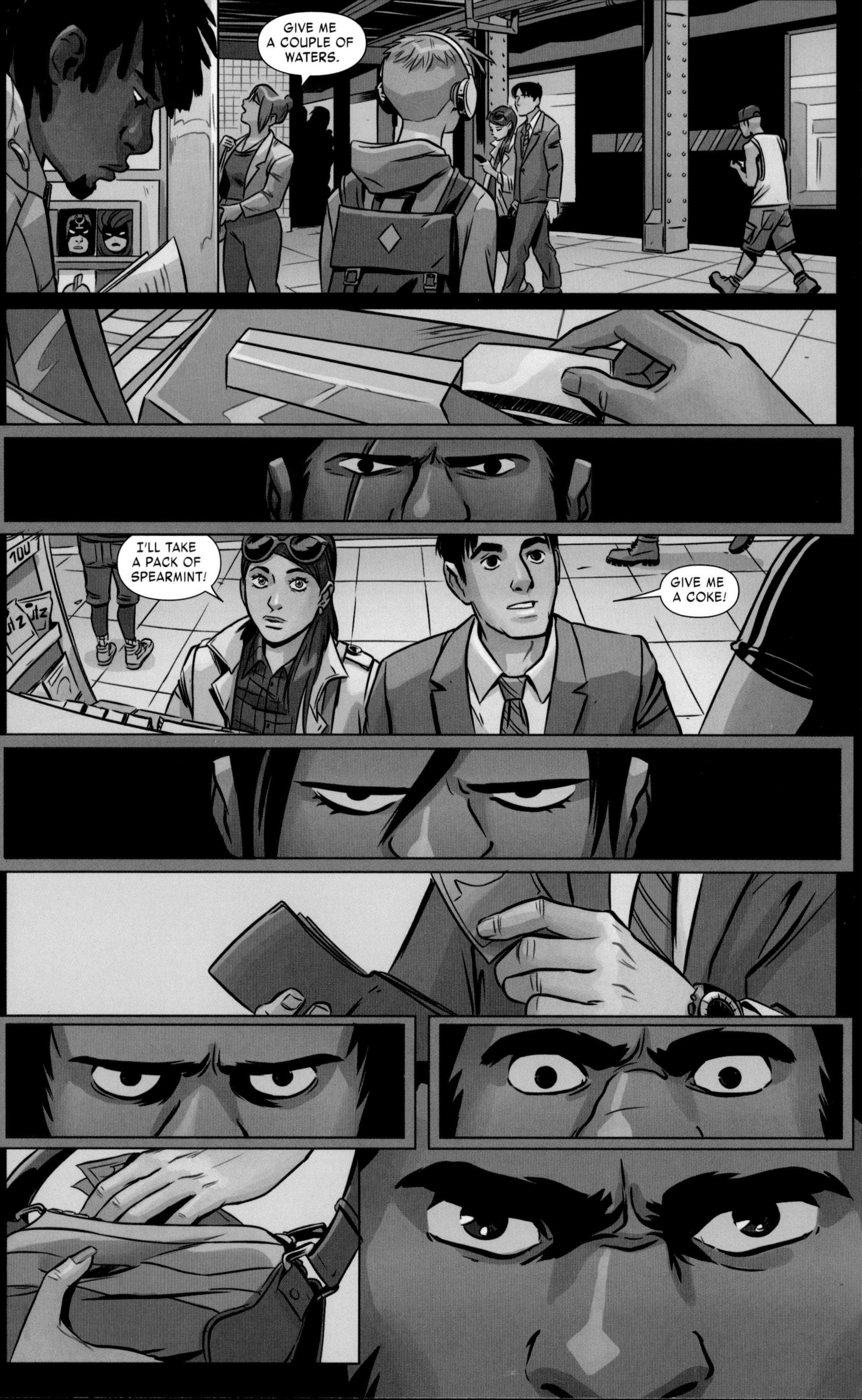
GIVE ME A COUPLE OF WATERS.
I'LL TAKE A PACK OF SPEARMINT!
GIVE ME A COKE!

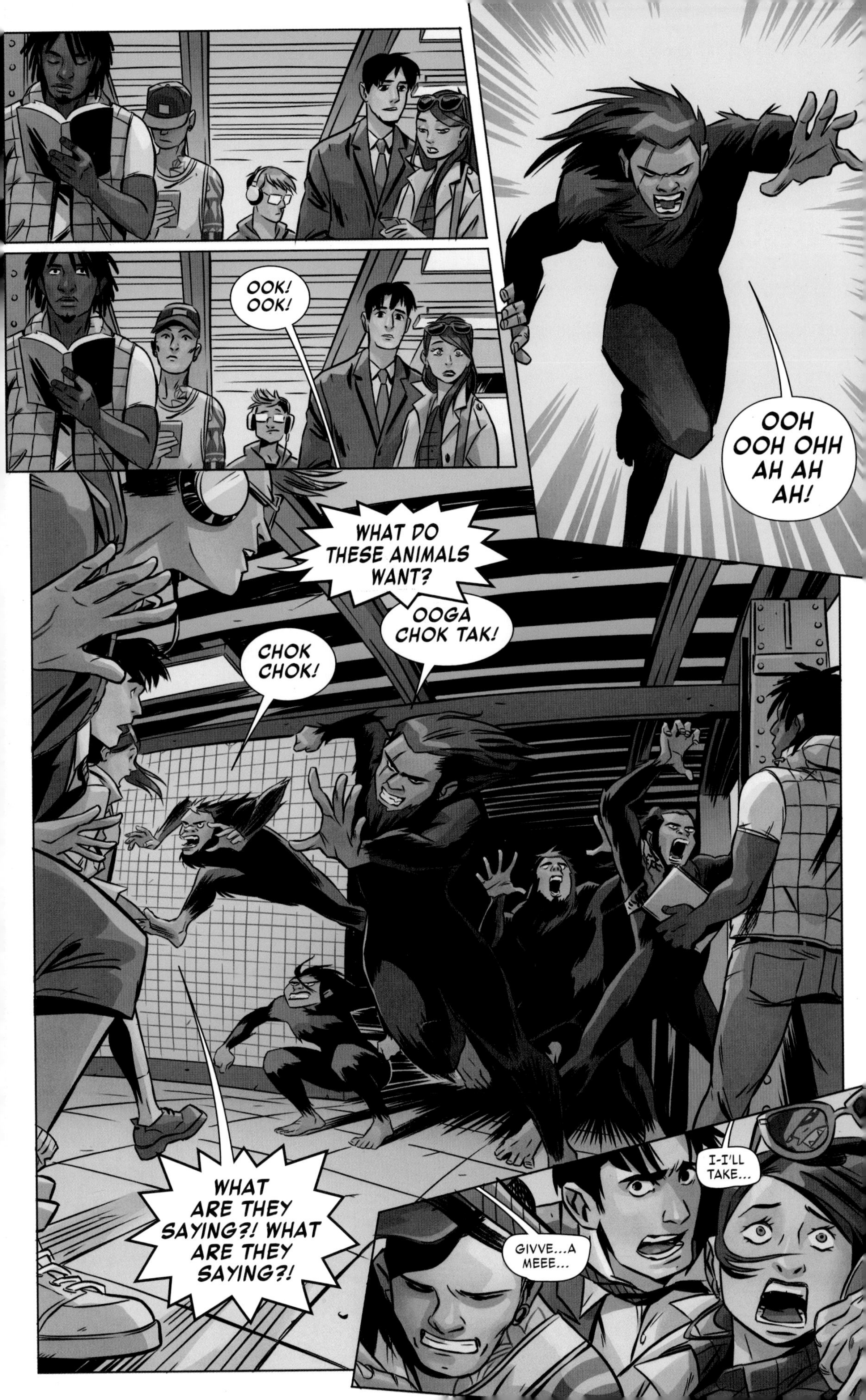
OOK! OOK!
OOH OOH OHH AH AH AH!
WHAT DO THESE ANIMALS WANT?
OOGA CHOK TAK!
CHOK CHOK!
WHAT ARE THEY SAYING?! WHAT ARE THEY SAYING?!
I-I'LL TAKE...
GIVVE...A MEEE...

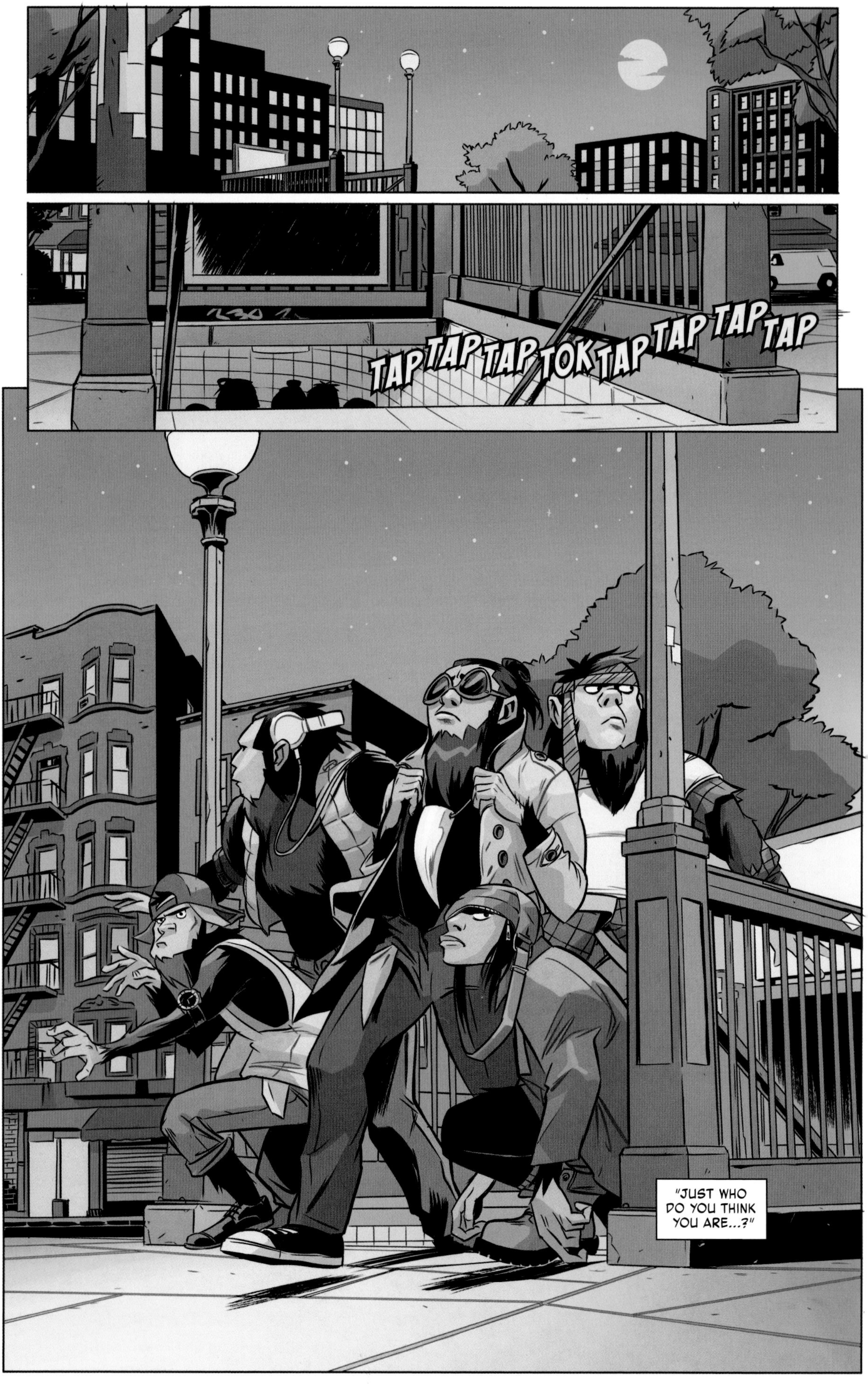
TAP TAP TAP TOK TAP TAP TAP TAP
"JUST WHO DO YOU THINK YOU ARE...?"

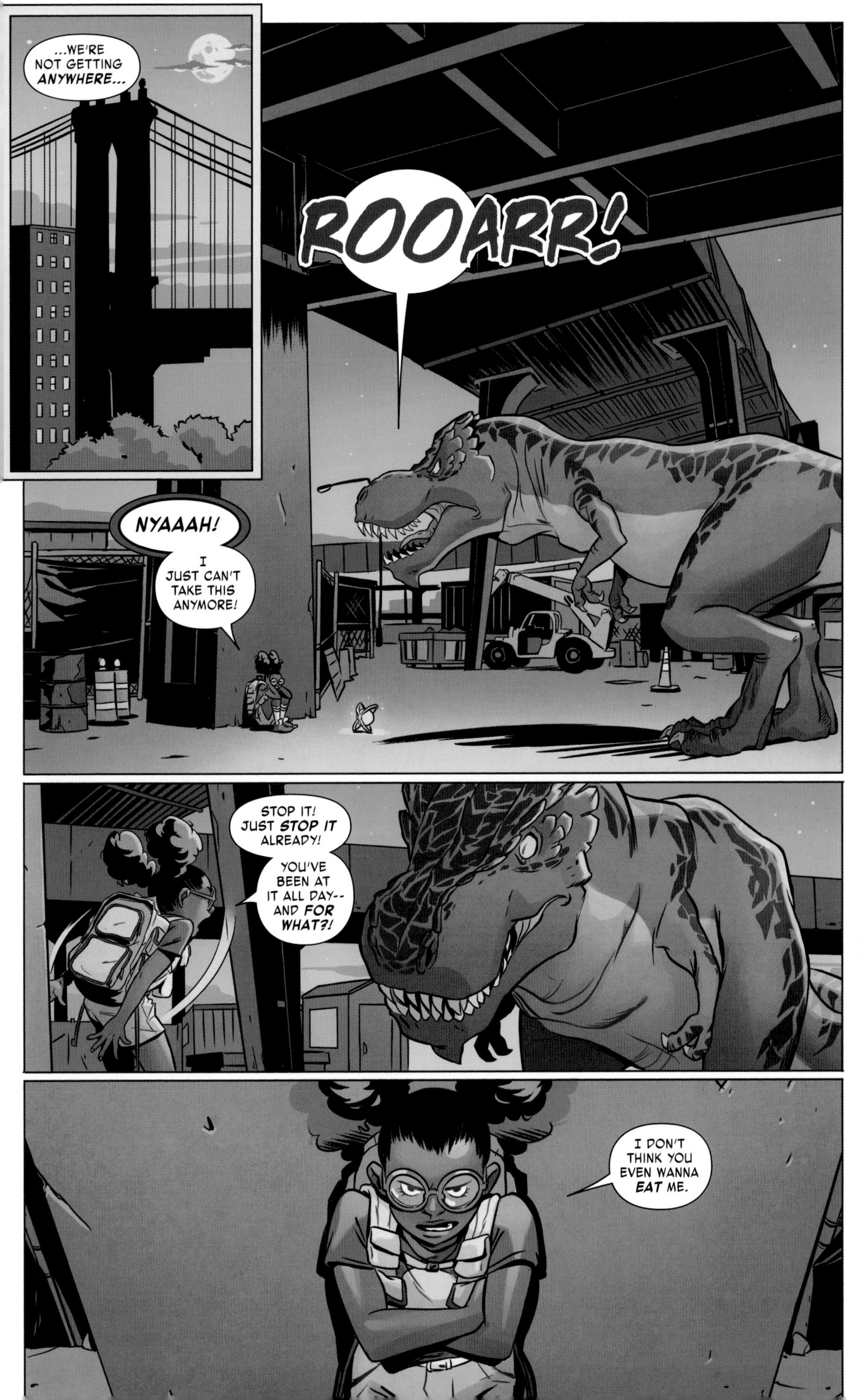
...WE'RE NOT GETTING ANYWHERE...
ROOARR!
NYAAAH!
I JUST CAN'T TAKE THIS ANYMORE!
STOP IT! JUST STOP IT ALREADY!
YOU'VE BEEN AT IT ALL DAY-- AND FOR WHAT?!
I DON'T THINK YOU EVEN WANNA EAT ME.

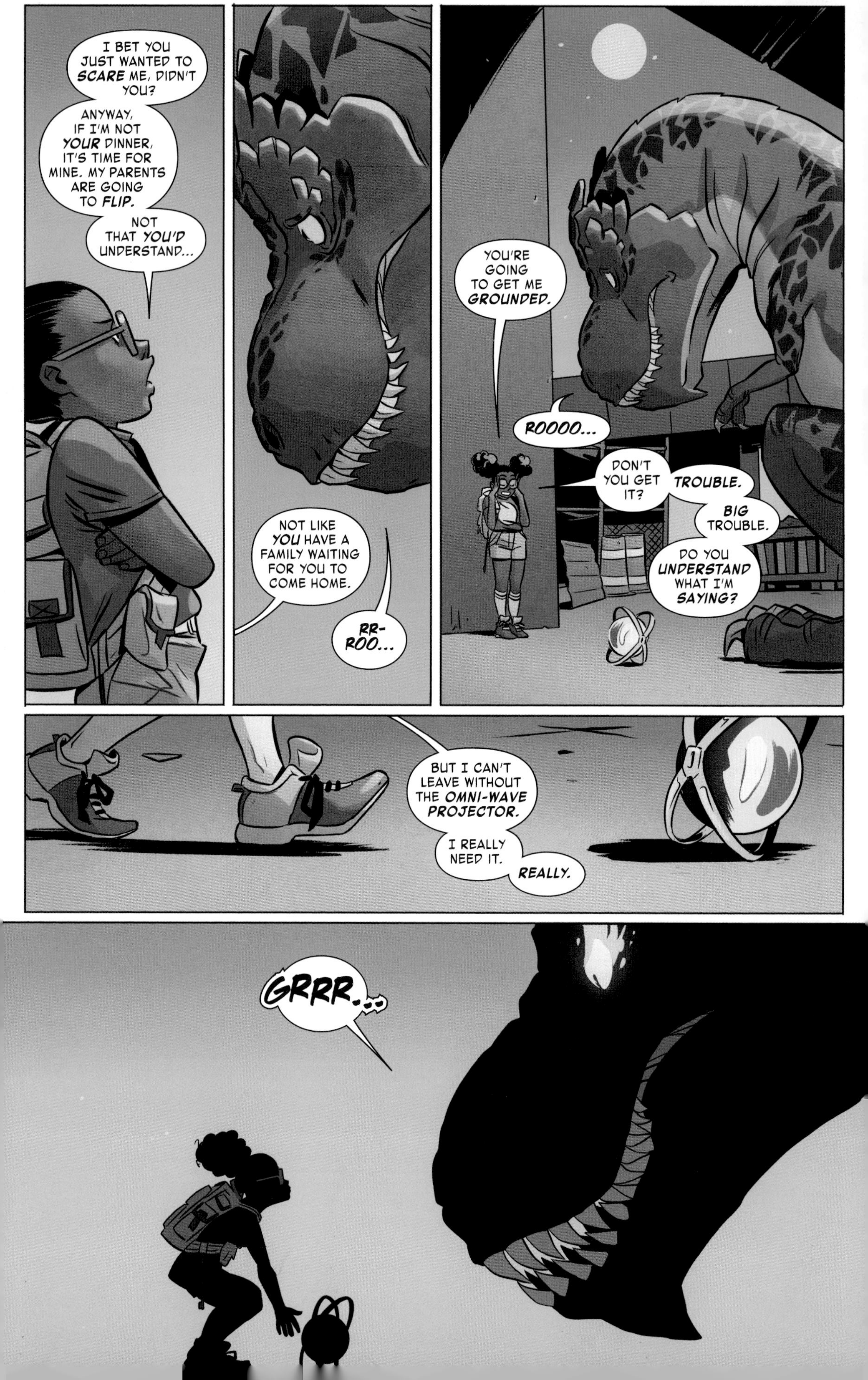
I BET YOU JUST WANTED TO SCARE ME, DIDN'T YOU?
ANYWAY, IF I'M NOT YOUR DINNER, IT'S TIME FOR MINE. MY PARENTS ARE GOING TO FLIP.
NOT THAT YOU'D UNDERSTAND...
NOT LIKE YOU HAVE A FAMILY WAITING FOR YOU TO COME HOME.
RR-ROO...
YOU'RE GOING TO GET ME GROUNDED.
ROOOO...
DON'T YOU GET IT?
TROUBLE.
BIG TROUBLE.
DO YOU UNDERSTAND WHAT I'M SAYING?
BUT I CAN'T LEAVE WITHOUT THE OMNI-WAVE PROJECTOR.
I REALLY NEED IT.
REALLY.
GRRR...

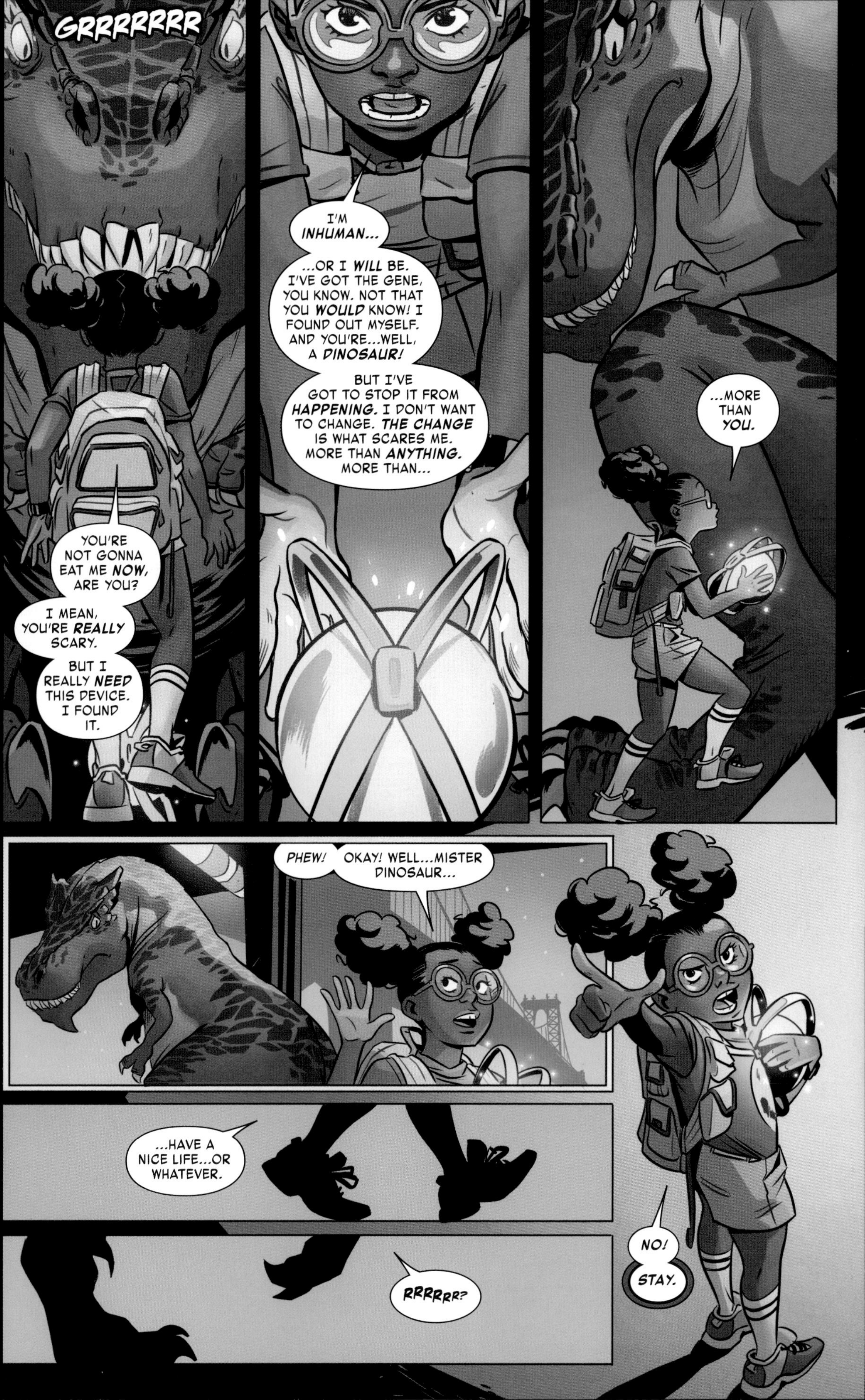
GRRRRRRR
YOU'RE NOT GONNA EAT ME NOW, ARE YOU?
I MEAN, YOU'RE REALLY SCARY.
BUT I REALLY NEED THIS DEVICE. I FOUND IT.
I'M INHUMAN...
...OR I WILL BE. I'VE GOT THE GENE, YOU KNOW. NOT THAT YOU WOULD KNOW! I FOUND OUT MYSELF. AND YOU'RE...WELL, A DINOSAUR!
BUT I'VE GOT TO STOP IT FROM HAPPENING. I DON'T WANT TO CHANGE. THE CHANGE IS WHAT SCARES ME. MORE THAN ANYTHING. MORE THAN...
...MORE THAN YOU.
PHEW!
OKAY! WELL...MISTER DINOSAUR...
...HAVE A NICE LIFE...OR WHATEVER.
RRRRRR?
NO!
STAY.

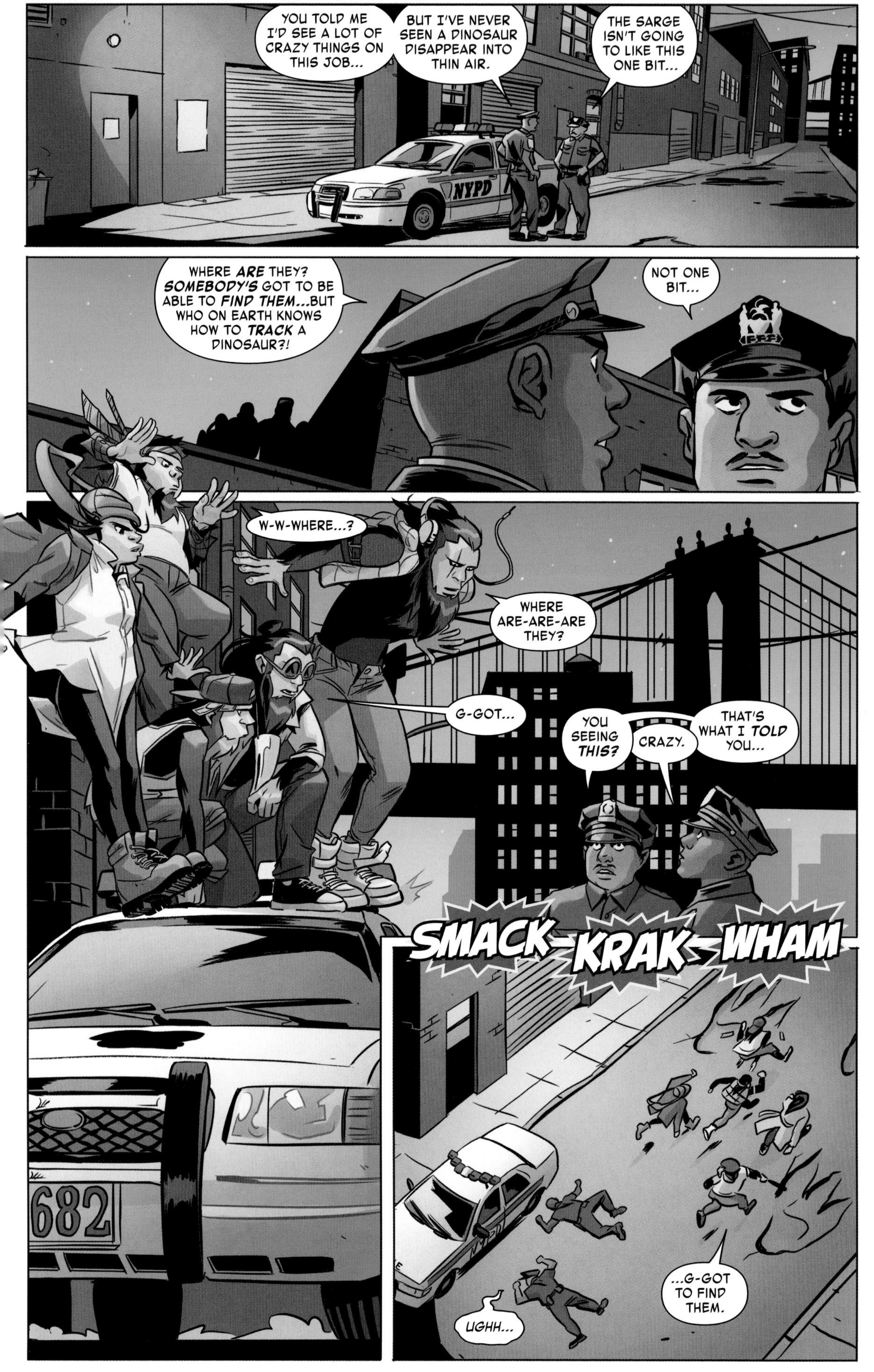
YOU TOLD ME I'D SEE A LOT OF CRAZY THINGS ON THIS JOB...
BUT I'VE NEVER SEEN A DINOSAUR DISAPPEAR INTO THIN AIR.
THE SARGE ISN'T GOING TO LIKE THIS ONE BIT...
NYPD
WHERE ARE THEY? SOMEBODY'S GOT TO BE ABLE TO FIND THEM...BUT WHO ON EARTH KNOWS HOW TO TRACK A DINOSAUR?!
NOT ONE BIT...
W-W-WHERE...?
WHERE ARE-ARE-ARE THEY?
G-GOT...
YOU SEEING THIS?
CRAZY.
THAT'S WHAT I TOLD YOU...
682
SMACK
KRAK
WHAM
...G-GOT TO FIND THEM.
UGHH...

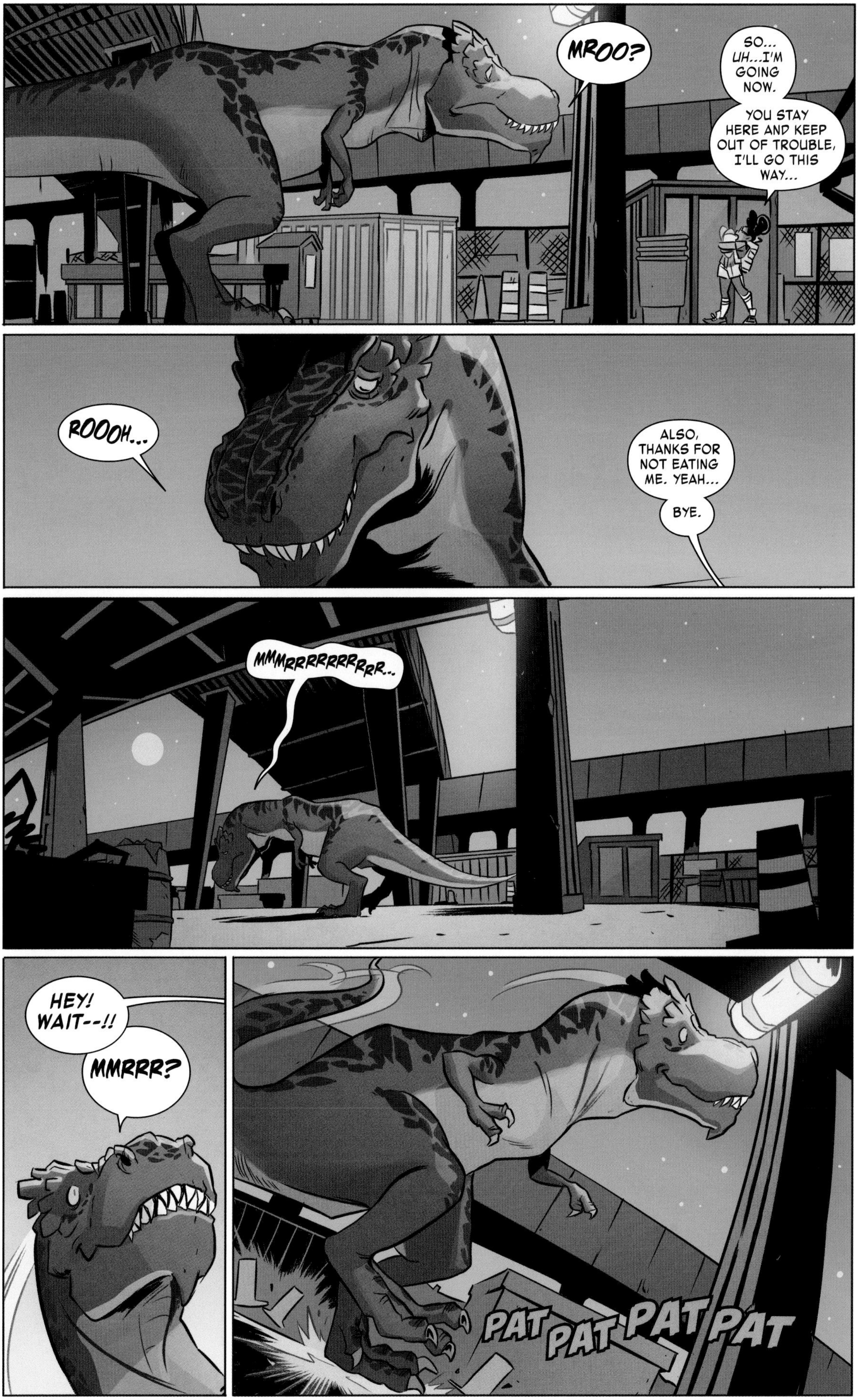
MROO?
SO... UH...I'M GOING NOW.
YOU STAY HERE AND KEEP OUT OF TROUBLE, I'LL GO THIS WAY...
ROOOH...
ALSO, THANKS FOR NOT EATING ME. YEAH...
BYE.
MMMRRRRRRRRRR...
HEY! WAIT--!!
MMRRR?
PAT PAT PAT PAT

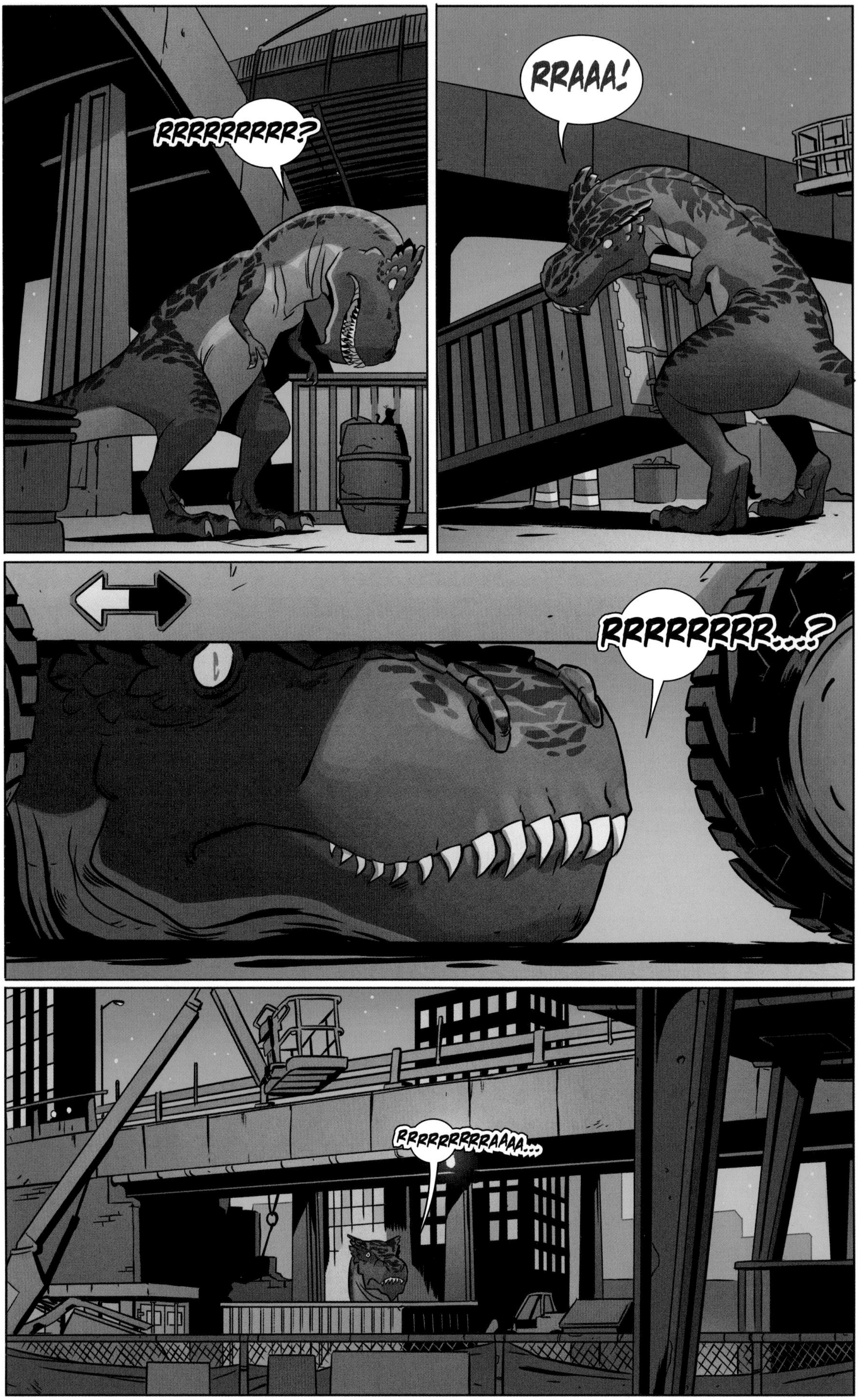
RRRRRRRRR?
RRAAA!
RRRRRRRR...?
RRRRRRRRRAAAA...

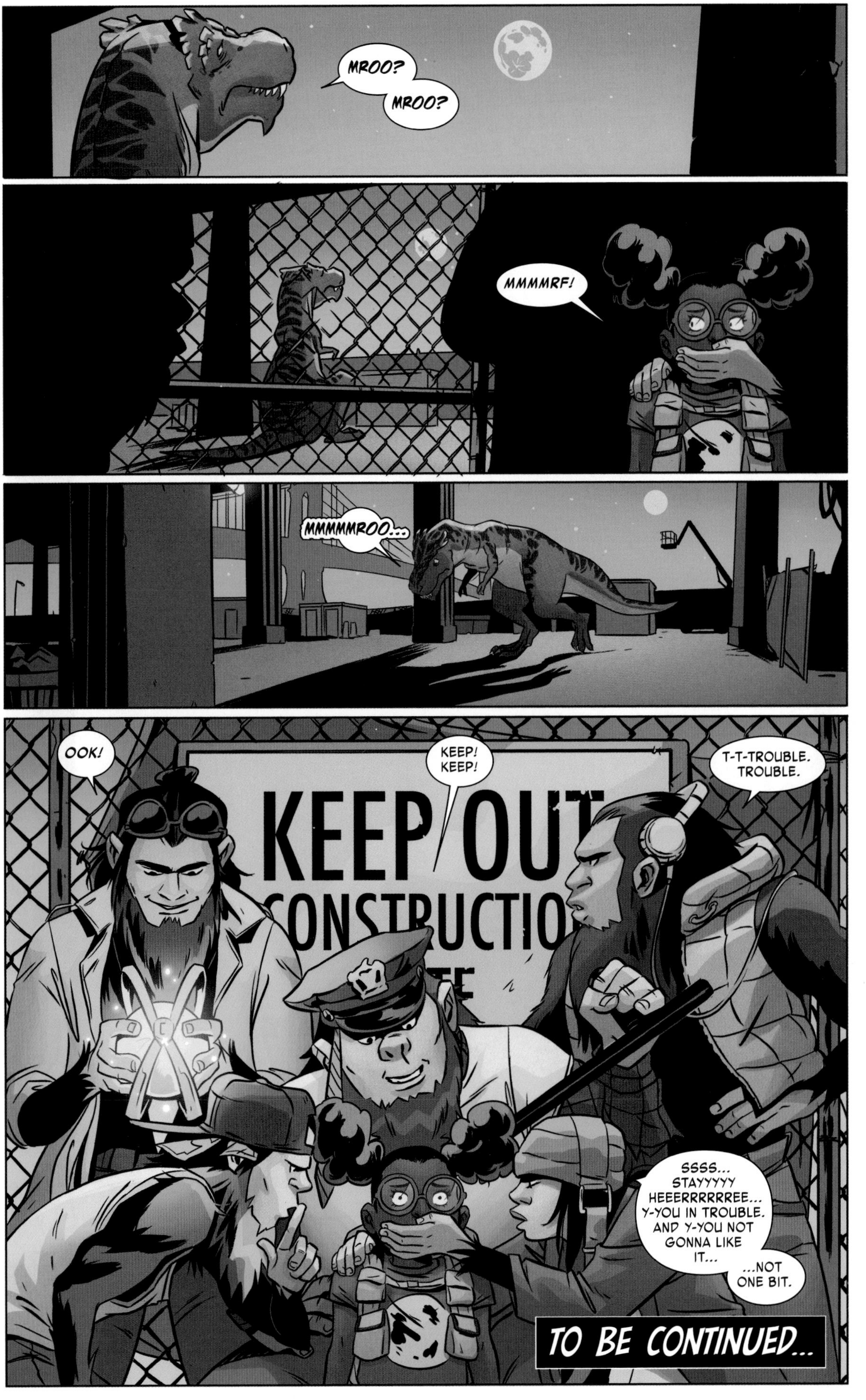
MROO?
MROO?
MMMMRF!
MMMMMROO...
OOK!
KEEP! KEEP!
KEEP OUT
CONSTRUCTIO
T-T-TROUBLE. TROUBLE.
SSSS... STAYYYYY HEEERRRRRREE... Y-YOU IN TROUBLE. AND Y-YOU NOT GONNA LIKE IT...
...NOT ONE BIT.
TO BE CONTINUED...

MOON GIRL AND DEVIL DINOSAUR™

COLLECT THEM ALL!

Set of 6 Hardcover Books ISBN: 978-1-5321-4007-5

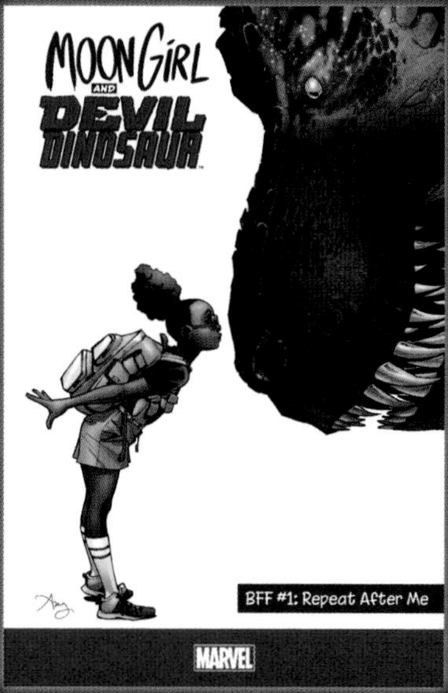
MOON GIRL AND DEVIL DINOSAUR
BFF #1: Repeat After Me
MARVEL

Hardcover Book ISBN
978-1-5321-4008-2

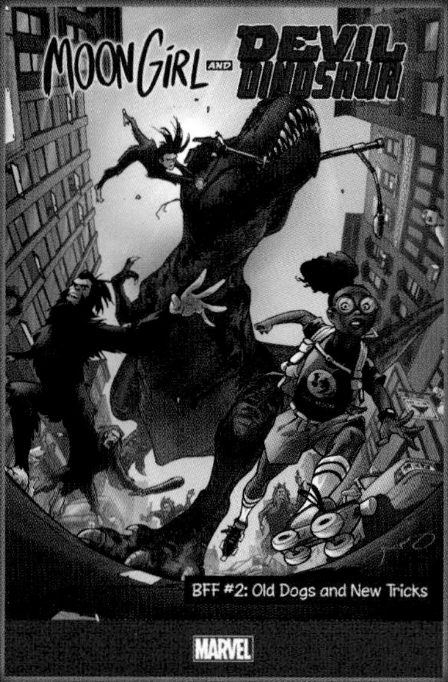
MOON GIRL AND DEVIL DINOSAUR
BFF #2: Old Dogs and New Tricks
MARVEL

Hardcover Book ISBN
978-1-5321-4009-9

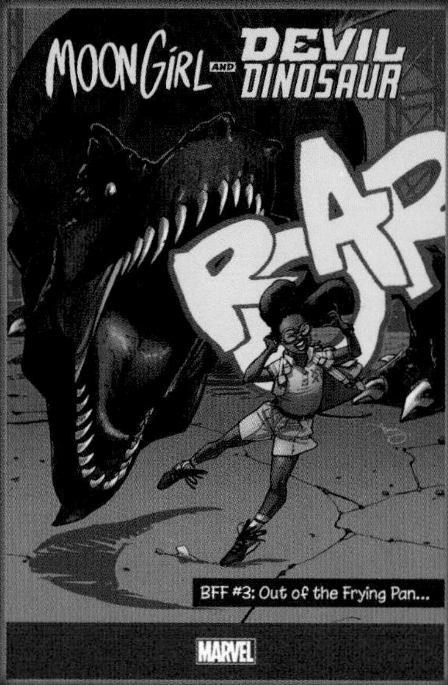
MOON GIRL AND DEVIL DINOSAUR
BFF #3: Out of the Frying Pan...
MARVEL

Hardcover Book ISBN
978-1-5321-4010-5

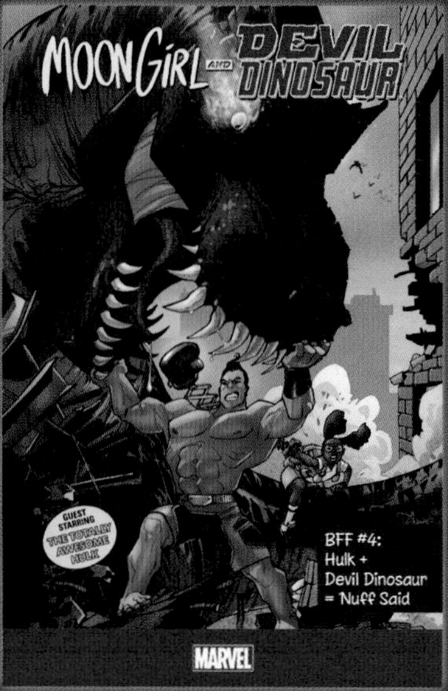
MOON GIRL AND DEVIL DINOSAUR
GUEST STARRING THE TOTALLY AWESOME HULK
BFF #4: Hulk + Devil Dinosaur = 'Nuff Said
MARVEL

Hardcover Book ISBN
978-1-5321-4011-2

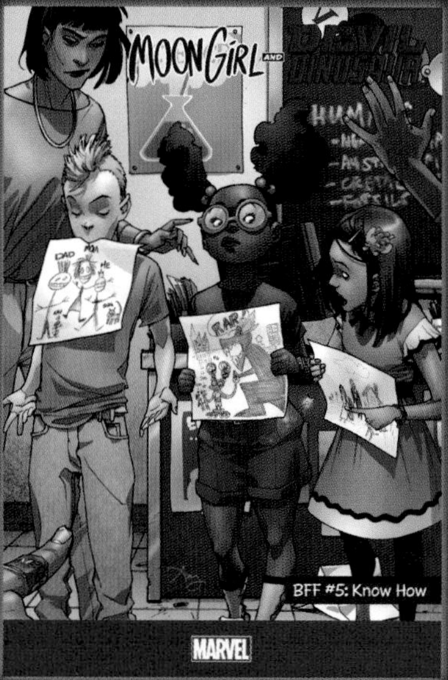
MOON GIRL AND DEVIL DINOSAUR
BFF #5: Know How
MARVEL

Hardcover Book ISBN
978-1-5321-4012-9

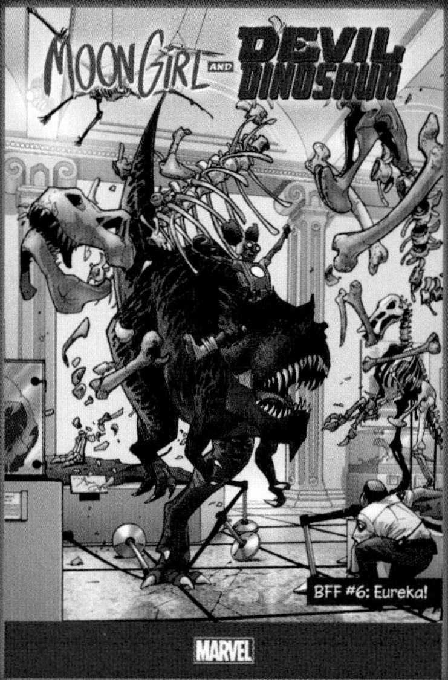
MOON GIRL AND DEVIL DINOSAUR
BFF #6: Eureka!
MARVEL

Hardcover Book ISBN
978-1-5321-4013-6